For Joshua with lots of love – D.G.

To Carole XX – A.B.

BLOOMSBURY CHILDREN'S BOOKS
Bloomsbury Publishing Plc
50 Bedford Square, London, WC1B 3DP, UK

BLOOMSBURY, BLOOMSBURY CHILDREN'S BOOKS and the Diana logo are trademarks of Bloomsbury Publishing Plc

First published in Great Britain 2018 by Bloomsbury Publishing Plc

Text copyright © Debi Gliori 2018
Illustration copyright © Alison Brown 2018

Debi Gliori and Alison Brown have asserted their rights under the Copyright, Design and Patents Act, 1988,
to be identified as the Author and Illustrator of this work.

A catalogue record for this book is available from the British Library

ISBN: HB: 978 1 4088 9219 0; PB: 978 1 4088 9221 3; eBook: 978 1 4088 9220 6

2 4 6 8 10 9 7 5 3 1

Printed in China by Leo Paper Products, Heshan, Guangdong

All papers used by Bloomsbury Publishing Plc are natural, recyclable products from
wood grown in well managed forests. The manufacturing processes conform to
the environmental regulations of the country of origin.

To find out more about our authors and books visit www.bloomsbury.com and sign up for our newsletters

Little Owl's First Day

Debi Gliori · Alison Brown

BLOOMSBURY
CHILDREN'S BOOKS

LONDON   OXFORD   NEW YORK   NEW DELHI   SYDNEY

Little Owl opened his eyes,
s-t-r-e-t-c-h-e-d his wings and yawned.

"Time to wake up," said Mummy Owl.
"It's a Big Day today – your first day at school!
Are you feeling excited?"

"No?" said Mummy Owl.

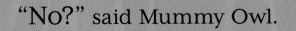

"NO," said Little Owl. "I don't like Big Days.
I want a small day. I want to stay at home
with you and Baby Owl."

Little Owl sat at the breakfast table,
slowly nibbling his Honey Seeded Numkins.

"Let's go, Little Owl," said Mummy.
"Don't forget your new owlbag."

"NO," said Little Owl. "I don't want to go.
I don't want an owlbag. I don't
want a Big Day, I want . . ."

Mummy Owl blinked.
"Tell you what," she said, "if we go now,
you can drive the pram."

"All the way over the bumpy bridge?" said Little Owl.

"All the way," said Mummy.

"Straight through the muddy puddles?"

"Straight through," Mummy sighed.

"Up the . . . *steep* . . . hill?"
gasped Little Owl, pushing hard.

"To the very top,"
said Mummy.

"Helloooo, Little Owl.
Welcome to our school,"
said Miss Oopik. "We're going
to have such a lovely time."

"When will you come back?"
Little Owl whispered in Mummy's ear.
"Very soon," Mummy Owl whispered back,
giving Little Owl a big hug.

"Come on, Little Owl," said Miss Oopik.
"Let's go and build a **rocket**."

"NO, thank you," said Little Owl.
"I want . . .

". . . to fly on a rocket with

Mummy and Baby Owl."

Today they'll be going to the moon
without me, he thought.

"Let's put on an apron
and do some painting,"
said Miss Oopik. "I bet
you're really good
at that."

Little Owl painted a picture of Mummy and Baby Owl
on a rocket. They were both covered in paint.
By the time he had finished, so was Little Owl.

"What a lovely picture!"
said Miss Oopik. "Let's pin it
on the wall, wash your
wings and then play with
the musical instruments."

"NO, thank you,"
said Little Owl.
"I really want . . .

". . . to go and play drums with Mummy and Baby Owl."

Today they'll be making LOTS of noise with the Big Beast Band – but without me, he thought.

"Come and see what we can find
in the sandpit," said Miss Oopik.
"Maybe you can give Tiny Owl
a hand with her castle?"

Little Owl liked helping Tiny Owl
with the fiddly bits.

"What clever owls!" said Miss Oopik.
"What an amazing castle.
Shall we try some water play next?"

"NO, thank you,"
said Little Owl.
"I want . . .

" . . . to splash water everywhere with Mummy and Baby Owl."

Today, they'll be sailing our pirate ship without me, he thought.

"Snack time!" said Miss Oopik. "Let's have
a look and see what's in our owlbags."
Little Owl opened his and found a home-made
seed cookie and a drawing from Mummy.

Little Owl shared his cookie
with Tiny Owl. And Tiny Owl
shared her squishy nut cake
with Little Owl. Very soon,
Little Owl began to
feel **much** better.

"We do **flying** next,"
said Tiny Owl.
"You'll **love** it!"

She was right.

Little Owl swooped and soared, he glided
and flapped, and for a whole hour he forgot
entirely about Mummy and Baby Owl.
Little Owl felt fantastic!

"Everyone on their leaf," said Miss Oopik.
"It's time for a story."

Little Owl helped
choose the book.

He snuggled up to Miss Oopik and
helped turn the pages.
He even joined in with the noises.

And when the story was finished . . .

. . . there were Mummy
and Baby Owl waiting
to take him home.

"What did you and Baby Owl
do while I was at school?"
yawned Little Owl.

"Oh, nothing much," said Mummy.
"I baked a cake and Baby Owl had a little nap.
What did you do all morning?"

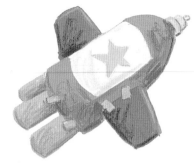

But Little Owl didn't say anything because Little Owl was fast asleep, tired out after his Very Big Day.